SAVIOUR PIROTTA was born in Malta, where he
began his career writing children's plays for radio. He moved
to the United Kingdom in 1981, and is now a popular storyteller
visiting schools around the country. His previous books include
Solomon's Secret (Methuen), *Pirates and Treasure* (Wayland)
and *Tales from Around the World* (Puffin). His first
book for Frances Lincoln was *Little Bird*.

NILESH MISTRY was born in Bombay, India. He came to
Britain in 1975 and studied at Harrow School of Art and
Central St Martin's School of Art. He has illustrated several children's
books, including *The Illustrated Book of Myths* (Dorling Kindersley),
Ghostly Haunts (Pavilion), the *Minnie* series (Longman)
and a new edition of *Alice in Wonderland* (OUP).

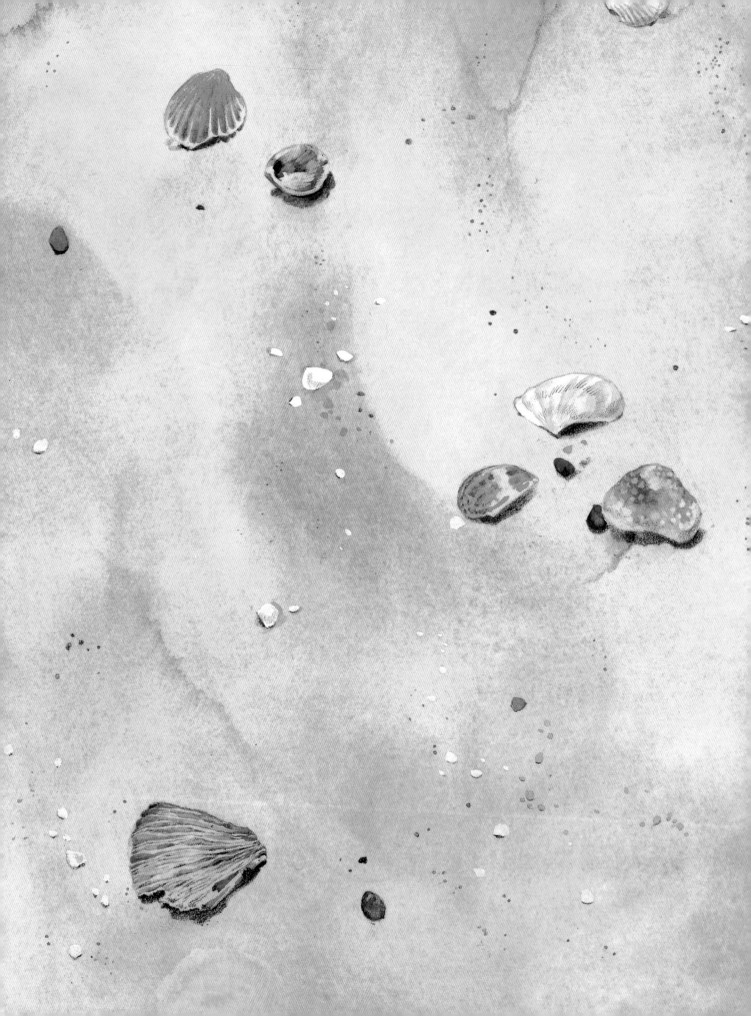

For Fiona and Aimée ~ S.P.

For Balkrishna and Rasik Mistry ~ N.M.

STORY BASED ON AN ORIGINAL IDEA BY YUKKI YAURA

Turtle Bay copyright © Frances Lincoln Limited 1997
Text copyright © Saviour Pirotta 1997
Illustrations copyright © Nilesh Mistry 1997
The right of Nilesh Mistry to be identified as the illustrator of this work has
been asserted by him in accordance with the Copyright, Designs and Patents Act,
1988 (United Kingdom).

First published in Great Britain in 1997 by Frances Lincoln Limited,
4 Torriano Mews, Torriano Avenue, London NW5 2RZ

First paperback edition 1998

British Library Cataloguing in Publication Data available on request

ISBN hardback 0-7112-1161-2
ISBN paperback 0-7112-1168-X

Printed in Hong Kong

1 3 5 7 9 8 6 4 2

Turtle Bay

SAVIOUR PIROTTA

Illustrated by NILESH MISTRY

FRANCES LINCOLN

TARO and Jiro-San were friends.

Jiro-San showed Taro how to feed crabs with pieces
of rotten fish. He taught him to dive for beautiful sponges.
When the sea was too rough for swimming, he trained
him to sit very still and watch the sea-horses swim around
the seaweed in the deeper rock pools.

Taro's sister, Yuko, didn't like Jiro-San very much.
"He's weird," she said. "Last year my friends
saw him sweeping the beach with a broom."
"No, he's not," said Taro. "He's old and wise,
and full of wonderful secrets."

One day, Taro found Jiro-San sitting on a big rock.

"What are you doing?" he asked.

"I am listening," said Jiro-San. "The wind is bringing me a message." Taro sat on the rock and listened. But all he could hear was the seagulls crying.

"Ah," said Jiro-San at last. "Now I understand . . . My old friends are coming."

"Who are your old friends?" asked Taro.

"You'll see," said Jiro-San.

Next day, Jiro-San brought two brooms and handed one to Taro.

"For sweeping the beach," he said.

Taro's heart sank. Yuko was right after all - Jiro-San was weird.

"There's a lot of rubbish and broken glass on the beach,"
Jiro-San explained. "My friends won't come if there is broken glass.
They know they'll get hurt."

The two friends swept the beach from one end to the other.
They collected all the rubbish and put it in Jiro-San's old cart.
Soon the beach was cleaner than it had been all summer.

Jiro-San looked pleased.

"Meet me by the big rock tonight," he told Taro.

Taro ate his supper as fast as he could.

"You seem in a big hurry," said his mother.

"I am," said Taro. "Jiro-San's old friends are coming."

"Who are they?" his mother wanted to know.

"It's a secret," said Taro.

"What kind of secret?" Yuko asked.

Taro didn't answer. He washed his hands and went out to find Jiro-San.

"Look," said the old man, pointing out to sea.
Taro saw a school of dolphins riding the waves.
"Are they your old friends?" he asked.
"No," said Jiro-San. "Perhaps they will come
tomorrow night."

Taro waited patiently all the next day. In the evening he met Jiro-San again. This time, the old man had brought his old boat out of the shed. Jiro-San picked up the oars and they pushed out to sea.

After a while, the old man said, "We've got company." Taro watched in amazement as a huge whale flicked her tail up out of the water. She had a young one swimming beside her.

"Are they your old friends?" Taro asked.

"They're friends," said Jiro-San, "but not the old friends I meant. Maybe they will come tomorrow."

The next evening, Jiro-San was in his boat again.

"Where are we going?" Taro wanted to know.

"Over there," said Jiro-San. He rowed out to a secret cove on a little island. There Taro saw three large fishes with swords for snouts.

"Are they your old friends?" Taro asked.

"All fish are my friends," said Jiro-San. "But these aren't my old friends. They seem to be late this year. Perhaps they are not coming at all."

"Don't be sad," Taro said. "Perhaps they'll get here tomorrow."

"Do you want to come and wait for Jiro-San's
old friends?" Taro asked Yuko after supper the next day.
Yuko wasn't doing anything, so she followed Taro to
the big rock, kicking the sand as she walked.

"Ssshh," said Jiro-San. "I think they're here at last."
Yuko and Taro saw a dark shape moving towards the shore.
It was huge and bobbed up and down on the water like an
enormous cork.

At last the children could see what it was - a turtle!
"She's coming to lay her eggs on our beach,"
said Jiro-San proudly.

The turtle scrambled ashore
and started digging with her flippers.
When the hole was deep enough, she laid
almost a hundred round, creamy-coloured eggs
in the nest. Then she filled in the hole with her
hind flippers, flung more sand over it with her
front flippers, and hurried back to the sea.
"She is going to tell the others," said Jiro-San.
"What is she going to tell them?" asked Yuko.
"That the beach is safe," said Taro happily.

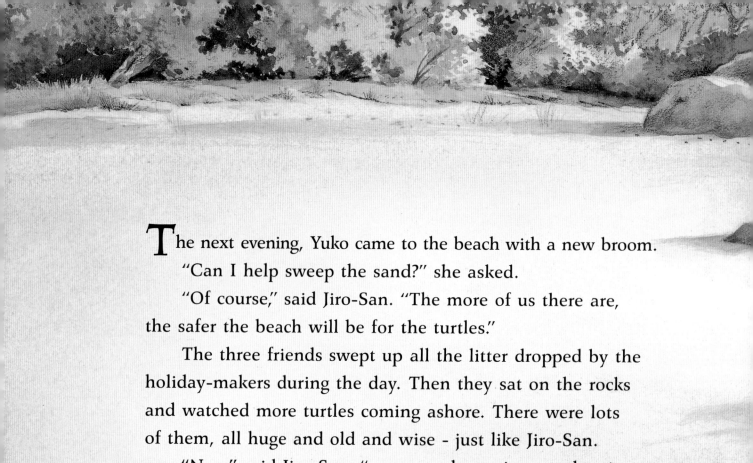

The next evening, Yuko came to the beach with a new broom.

"Can I help sweep the sand?" she asked.

"Of course," said Jiro-San. "The more of us there are, the safer the beach will be for the turtles."

The three friends swept up all the litter dropped by the holiday-makers during the day. Then they sat on the rocks and watched more turtles coming ashore. There were lots of them, all huge and old and wise - just like Jiro-San.

"Now," said Jiro-San, "you must be patient, and wait until you hear from me again."

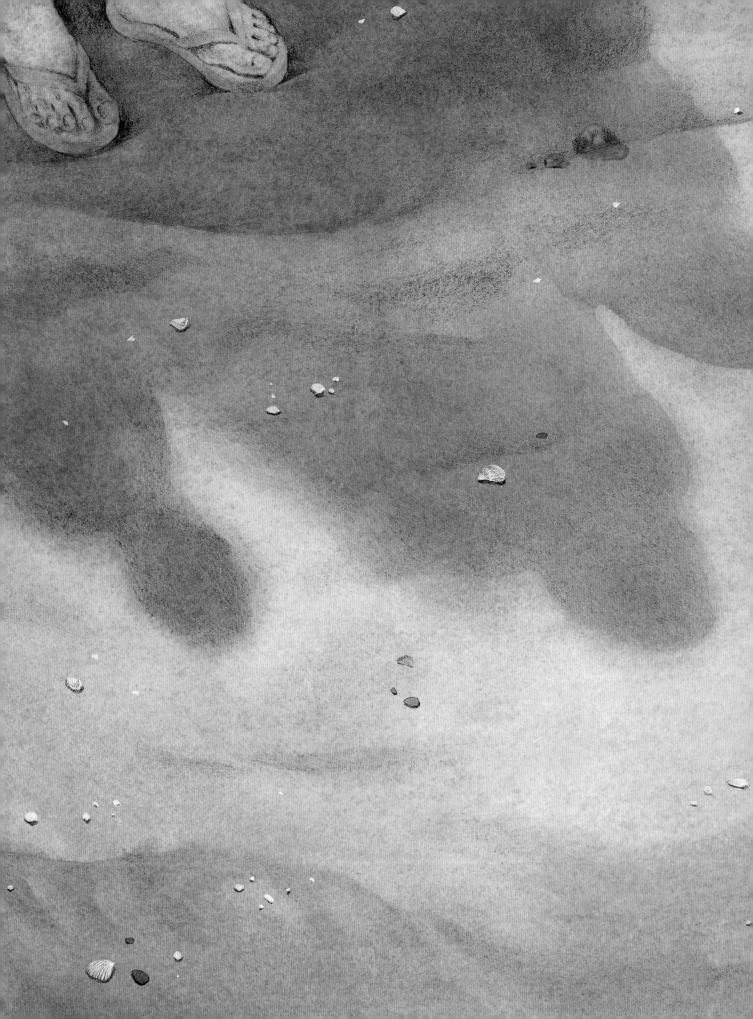

Eight weeks later, Jiro-San told the children to meet him at dusk.

"Sit on the rocks, please," he said, "and watch the ground."

The children looked and waited for what seemed like hours.
As the moon rose, they saw something moving under the sand -
something small and fast and eager.

"It's a baby turtle!" cried Taro. "The eggs have hatched!"

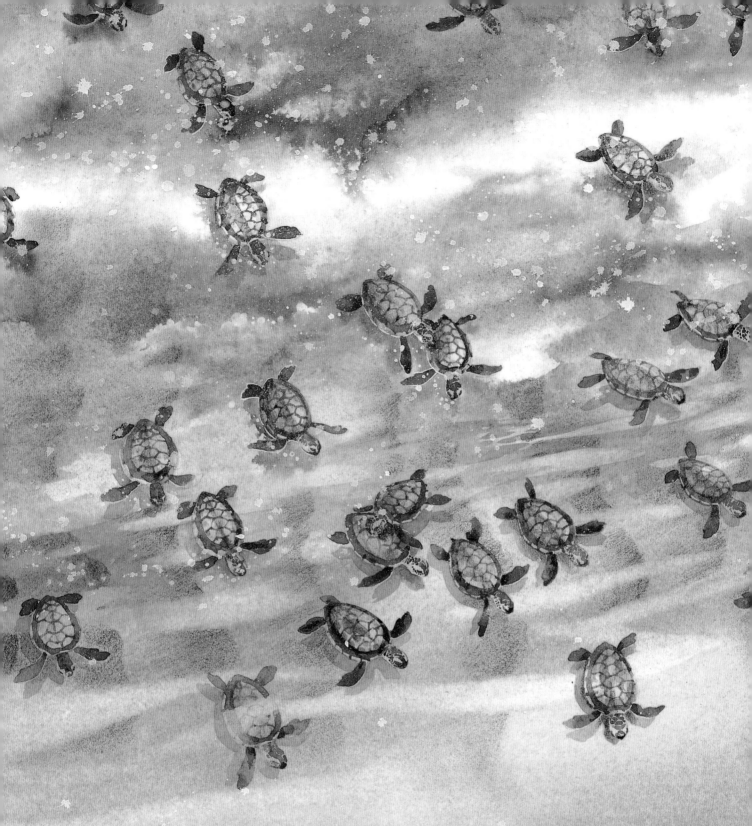

Soon the beach was full of baby turtles. There were
hundreds of them, all scuttling down to the sea.
The children couldn't believe their eyes.

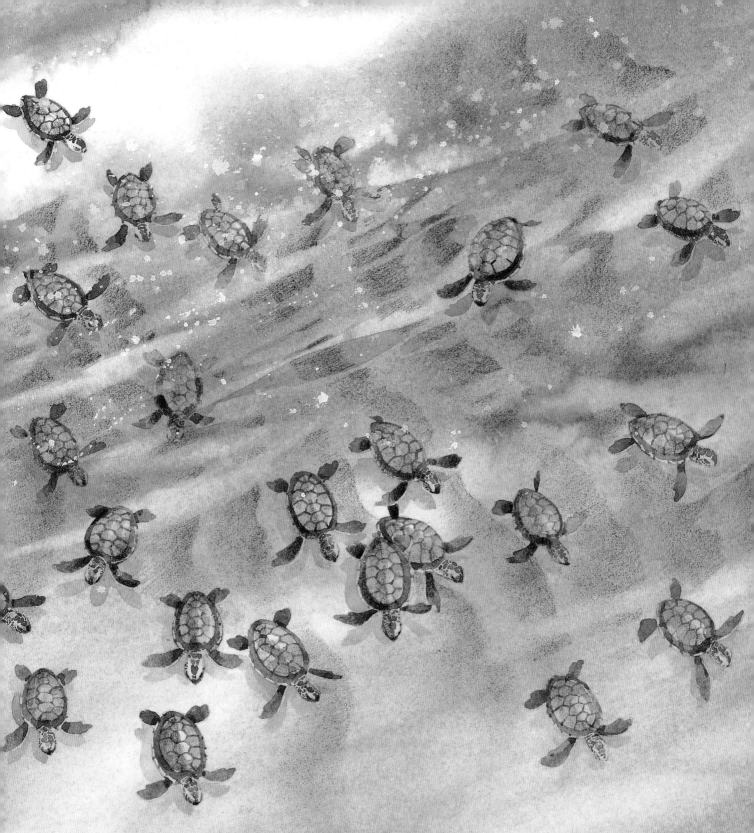

"Jiro-San is not crazy after all, is he?" Taro whispered to Yuko.
"No," said Yuko. "He is old and wise ... and full of
wonderful secrets!"

About Sea Turtles

Jiro-San's old friends are loggerhead turtles, one of seven different kinds of turtles living in the sea. Although turtles are born on dry land and breathe air, they spend most of their lives swimming in the warm oceans, feeding on sea grasses, crabs, shrimps and shells. Like tortoises and terrapins, they have bodies that are protected by armour made of bones and horny shell.

When the weather is warm, loggerhead turtles migrate to shallow water to mate, and the females come ashore at night to lay their eggs on sandy beaches, using the same places that have been used for centuries.

Each female digs a bucket-sized pit with her flippers. Her eggs - 100 or more - have leathery shells so they will not break as they plop into the nest. She covers the nest with sand to hide it from greedy creatures such as lizards.

The mother turtle cannot survive long on land, so she goes back to the sea and takes no further care of her family.

After two months, the eggs hatch and the baby turtles push their way up to the surface of the sand and scurry down to the water. They usually go by night, for by day sea-birds and other enemies might catch them. Once in the sea, they can live for over fifty years.

Except for large sharks, adult sea turtles do not have many enemies, but some human beings like to eat turtle meat and to make things out of their shells, and turtles sometimes get caught in fishing nets. People also like to build hotels and spend holidays on the beaches where turtles lay their eggs, so in those places turtles have become very rare.

Conservationists are now trying to help protect turtles and their breeding-grounds.

OTHER PICTURE BOOKS IN PAPERBACK
FROM FRANCES LINCOLN

GROWING PAINS
Jenny Stow

Poor baby Shukudu! It's hard trying to be a rhinoceros when you
have no horns. "Horns take time to grow," says his mother.
How Shukudu learns patience and gains his heart's desire is
portrayed with warmth and humour by Jenny Stow.

Suitable for National Curriculum English - Reading, Key Stage 1
Scottish Guidelines English Language - Reading, Levels A and B

ISBN 0-7112-1036-5   **£4.99**

THE SNOW WHALE
Caroline Pitcher *illustrated by* Jackie Morris

One November morning, when the hills are hump-backed
with snow, Laurie and Leo decide to build a snow whale. As they
shovel and pat and polish to bring the snow whale out of the hill,
the whale gradually takes on a life of its own.

Suitable for National Curriculum English - Reading, Key Stage 1
Scottish Guidelines English Language - Reading, Levels A and B

ISBN 0-7112-1093-4   **£4.99**

INDIGO AND THE WHALE
Joyce Dunbar *illustrated by* Geoffrey Patterson

A boy who longs to be a musician...a talking jackdaw...
a rainbow pipe with magical powers...The spellbinding story of Indigo,
who charms a whale with his pipe-playing and finds himself on a
momentous journey of discovery, will enchant young readers
with its colours and music of the deep.

Suitable for National Curriculum English-Reading, Key Stages 1 and 2
Scottish Guidelines English Language - Reading, Level B

ISBN 0-7112-1080-2   **£4.99**

Frances Lincoln titles are available from all good bookshops.

Prices are correct at time of publication, but may be subject to change.